*For the AllHealth staff and*

*Special thanks to cover artist, Charlie Beasley*

National Domestic Abuse Hotline 1-800-799-7233

Childhelp National Child Abuse Hotline 1-800-422-4453

# The Unkindness

By Noah Cole-Hassell

The year was 1694 in a small village within Massachusetts, and despite it being well into September it was swelteringly hot. The grass was a sickly dull brown; that cracked and snapped as it was walked upon. The heat had stripped it and most of the other vegetation of any of its once lively forest green color. Tensions were beginning to run as high in the village as the heat of the surrounding air. There were rumors floating around that this heat felt unnatural. Some whispered the witches slain in the trials the year before had cursed not just Salem, but all good Puritan homesteads. Others claimed it was the doing of the savages who refused to convert after King Philip's war.

However one member of the village remained unperturbed by such things. She was a beautiful slender girl of twelve, named Arabia. She had grown taller than even some of the boys in the village, although she still was just shy of five feet. She had piercing blue eyes that seemed to sparkle ever so slightly, bearing a striking resemblance to the early evening sky. They were filled with a rare inviting warmth that had a contradictory coldness behind them if you gaze long enough. Her hair was so great in length it touched the tops of her thighs and was a shining jet black that in the right light looked very much like the color of a raven, though she often hid it in her coif. Her skin was pale, almost on par with the sheen of an ivory figurine.

Arabia was a gentle and compassionate girl, but despite this she struggled to befriend the other children in the village. She didn't attend school and was illiterate, which in their village wasn't abnormal for young girls. Nevertheless other children found her strange and slightly off putting, for reasons lost even to themselves. While she never held contempt for the people of the village she also never felt connected to any of them. This extended even to her own father; for her mother had passed while giving birth to her, a fact her father would remind her of every day.

His name was Gideon. He was a moderately tall man, with a powerful build that he acquired from years of chopping down trees to sell for lumber to neighboring villages and towns. His arms were dauntingly thick with a coat of dark black hair that many would say gave him the appearance of a black bear, with the demeanor of a grizzly. His eyes were a shade of brown, reminiscent of freshly tanned leather. Gideon had a thick matted beard that often contained bits of whatever his previous meal consisted of. He often smelt of dried sweat, spirits, and freshly cut oak, a smell that never failed to make Arabia's stomach twist into knots upon his return every night.

He would frequently stumble in well after the sun had set, having used most of his day's pay to drown his misery while fueling Arabia's. If her chores were not completed to his liking, no matter how meaningless it may be, he would forcibly drag her out of bed and demand she do it over again whilst berating her uselessness. If she objected or even made the attempt to explain why it was not done to his liking he would strike her with the back of his hand or lash her on the back with a switch, saying, "She needed to honor her father," and, "what he does is mercy for the love he bared for her mother and she ought to be grateful!"

While his blows hurt, the real damage was from knowing that no matter what Arabia did, her father wasn't capable of loving her.

✳

One disturbingly warm night Arabia awoke in the earliest hours of the morning with a sharp jolt, and a lingering unknown and foreboding sense of panic. Her chest heaved heavily as she tried to catch her breath. She scanned the room half expecting to see her father, eyes glaring and full of wrath, yet as her sight adjusted to the surrounding darkness she saw nothing but the usual knick knacks. Their home was a humble house with only two rooms -- one bedroom where Arabia's father would sleep and the main area where they would take their evening supper and double as Arabia's sleeping quarters. She tried to remember what it was that woke her so violently; She had vague recollection of a rabid bear frothing from the mouth, onyx black wings that carried joy and yet had an air of sorrow beneath them. The last thing that the young girl could recall was a strange pyramid that had an utterly terrifying feeling of inevitability that started to send her into a panic where it was difficult to even breathe. After almost half an hour Arabia began to calm herself and think how silly she was for working herself up over nothing. It had been a dream nothing more, however she knew there would be no getting back to sleep.

She decided to get an early start on her chores, quietly setting about her tasks so as to not wake her father.

She ventured off to collect water from the village's well so she could make porridge to break their fast. The sun had not yet risen making it substantially cooler, much to Arabia's relief. Arabia made her way to the center of the village, a walk that would take no more than ten minutes. Along her way she breathed in the cool humid air, smelling the dew still on the surrounding vegetation and appreciating the quiet and calm of this hour. She arrived at the well, the panic and terror that had awoken her was a distant memory till she laid eyes on the center of the village.

The center was where the village would gather for big events or news. It was a fifty square foot dirt plot with a raised wooden platform at the farthest end from the well and just in front of the humble village church. Nothing about it seemed menacing on the surface, however Arabia began to tremble all over her body as sweat began to form on her palms and brow. She knew not what came over her but it was a profound sense of dread. Arabia drew a pail of water from the well and fled back home faster than she'd ever gone before. She sloshed almost half of the water out of the pail as she ran but she paid no mind, all she could think about was getting home.

On the eastern horizon the sun had finally begun to show its full self. The heat already began to feel overbearing and sapping of the moisture as well as people's motivation. The oddity to this being Arabia. She had found herself with a foreign vigor that had allowed her to make the morning meal, consisting of just simple porridge and a small loaf of day old bread. Her father awoke to the aroma of food ready on the table. Gideon gave a slightly unfamiliar grunt of approval, stating his lessons must finally be getting through to her. Arabia gave him a polite smile, too preoccupied with the haze of her own thoughts to pay his comment any mind.

As Gideon finished his meal, washing it down with his usual morning mug of beer, he then proceeded to gather his axe, gloves, and saw then set out for another day's work. Leaving Arabia wondering how she should spend her hours of freedom for the day. It would still be some time till the noon sun; nevertheless Arabia could already feel the scathing heat filling her home. There was a river not more than a mile from the village; it would be a perfect way to stave off the oppressing warmth. It was normally seen as a taboo by most puritans to trounce around in the forest, but the heat compelled Arabia to take the trip.

The noon sun was high in the sky by the time Arabia made it to the forest; the heat was normally approaching near unbearable levels as of late, nonetheless Arabia was mostly unbothered by it on this day. Her journey was pleasantly cool, for she was deeper in the woods than she had ever been. The trees even with most of their leaves missing, had acted as a blanket of shade till she came to the river. She chose a spot on the bank where the water was shallow enough for her to stand yet the water still moved with some urgency to it. She removed her leather shoes and wool socks and proceeded to soak her tired feet in the chilling and rejuvenating waters of the river.

Arabia had often been told to avoid the forest for it was supposed to be filled with savages, witches, evil spirits, and some said even the Devil himself. Yet, Arabia saw nothing of the sort. In fact as she smelled the oak trees and felt the invigorating breeze she had been filled with more peace and comfort than she ever did in the village. Even her father's Bible studies, to her shame, hadn't made her feel as close to God as she did here in the forest. It even made her recall her favorite piece of scripture:

"*Blessed be the man that trusteth in the Lord, and whose hope the Lord is. For he shall be as a tree that is planted by the water, which speadith out her roots by the river, and shall not feel when the heat cometh, but her leaf shall be green , and shall not care for the year of drought, neither shall cease from yielding fruit*"- Jeremiah 17: 7-8.

As she was contemplating all these conflicting thoughts and feelings, a series of sharp harsh cries flurried up. Snapping back into her present moment she whirled her head around, wildly looking for the source of the commotion; half afraid some malevolent spirit was about to pounce upon her. She soon spotted a small group of black birds flying in erratic, sharp, twisting patterns. Arabia counted four birds in total, and it appeared three of them were out to harm the frantic one in the lead. She noticed the lead black bird was slightly larger than its pursuers; however it mattered little against their numbers. She realized that it was a raven, who was being mercilessly harassed by crows. The raven struggled to flee; its desperation grew as it flew more wildly over head; diving then soaring up high, turning quickly to the left then back to the right.

Arabia began to feel the panic in the raven's movements; she too knew what that fear felt like and wanted nothing more than to sprout wings of her own and help. She quickly rose to her feet, shouting as loud as she could for the crows to leave the raven alone, but to no avail. Arabia saw the constitution of the raven begin to fail as it flew lower and lower, soon landing across the bank where the crows pecked and scratched it from the air. Seeing how helpless the poor and exhausted raven was saddened Arabia, but the relentless jackal-like nature of the crows brought her to wrath. She screamed with a primal ferocity that broke the crows focus on the downed raven. She found as many stones along the river as she could, and proceeded to launch them at the crows whilst marching across to the other bank to aid the raven. This turn of events shocked the crows so badly that they flew off into the tree line, out of range of Arabia's endless volley of stones. She whispered soft words of reassurance to the raven, which was too weak to resist her when she scooped it into her arms. She carried it in the same way a mother would carry a babe; letting the raven know they were now safe and she swore no more harm shall befall them.

Several hours had passed allowing the young raven to regain some strength and Arabia could see the life pouring back into the beautiful, energetic bird. Her feathers were such a deep black that they almost appeared blue in places. Her beak came to a straight point, and looked sharper than any blade Arabia had seen, yet the playful spark in her eyes told Arabia she could be trusted. She had come to the conclusion the raven she rescued was a young female that had gotten lost deep in the crows' territory. Arabia thought it was strange she would be on her own, especially at a young age, but didn't give it much thought beyond that.

Arabia's new companion had taken to roosting on her head or shoulder which would bring out a previously unheard of fit of giggles from the young girl. In turn, the young raven would mimic her with its own voice. Her new friend found a great deal of joy in putting twigs and small leaves in her hair; in vain Arabia would remove them only to find more placed elsewhere in her flowing black locks. Arabia had never thought a bird could be so delightful, let alone a raven!

Arabia felt compelled to think of a name for her new playmate. She went through a list of names to see if her friend would respond to any. She tried Delilah, Abigail, Mara, and Mary; all were met with the same indifference. Arabia furrowed her brow in concentration, for she wanted her new friend to have a name they both enjoyed; then it came to her, Brenna! It meant "little raven" and oddly this was the only name to gain her raven friend's attention, filling Arabia with a sense of pride and joy!

Smiling Arabia exclaimed "Brenna shall be your name!", which seemed to satisfy the small bird who would mimic the sound of her new name, which sounded eerily like Arabia's own voice.

*"Brenna!", "Brenna!", "Brenna!"*

Arabia's eyes widened as her mouth hung ajar; she hadn't expected an actual response! So wrapped up in the joy she was experiencing on this day, Arabia had lost track of time and dark would soon be setting in on her.

Arabia was so deeply engrossed in an odd sort of game of fetch with her new winged associate Brenna; that she remained ignorant to the sun sneaking behind the western horizon. Arabia would throw a twig up in the air and watch with pure glee as Brenna would catch the twig in her talons and proceed to pass it to her powerful yet precise beak then back again, ending with Brenna dropping it for Arabia to catch. This was such an astonishing game for the pair of them that it was well into dusk by the time either of them realized.

When Arabia finally began to take notice of the sun long since lost; dread soon consumed her. How would she find her way back in the dark? What if a beast of the night took her as she returned? What if she lost her way in the obscure and foreign dark of the woods? These thoughts started to bring tears to her eyes and she proceeded to drop down on her side and cry. Brenna was confused by the strange and harsh new noise her savior was making. It was nothing like her high squeals whilst playing, but was empty of the wildness of her cry when battling the crows.

Brenna landed on Arabia's petty coat with a softness unnoticed by Arabia. Brenna made gentle reassuring coos like her mother used to do for her in hopes this might sooth her but to little effect. Brenna then decided to hop, with grace and playfulness, directly on to Arabia's head.

In frustration Arabia snapped at Brenna telling her to "get off!" This caused Brenna to take to the nearby trees in fear and confusion. Realizing she frightened the little raven, she apologized profusely knowing poor Brenna could never understand her remorse. However as if comprehending entirely, Brenna swooped down to Arabia's shoulder and in an unspoken acceptance, she warmly nuzzled Arabia with her beak. This small act calmed Arabia allowing her to think clearly once again. She stood and dusted off her skirts, and told herself she was being childish. If she found her way into the forest, then she could find her way out. She looked to the sky and she saw smoke rising above the tree line and with a trial by fire, she tested this new found confidence. She went head first in the direction of where she saw the smoke with Brenna faithfully perched on her shoulder.

The journey home was at least two hours more than it had been when entering the forest. The dark made Arabia's pace slower than a snail going uphill, however that meant she had to really learn every twist, turn, and bend between the village and her peaceful river nook. After braving the unknown it was with a sigh of relief, Arabia had finally made it back to her village. Arabia turned to Brenna, whose head was playfully cocked to the side giving her the resemblance of a curious puppy. She thanked her for the wonderful day and accompanying her on her adventure home, but it was time to part ways for now. With a gentle push she sent Brenna off to the trees and hurried home, unaware that Brenna decided to shadow her new friend.

Arabia entered her home unbeknownst to her that a storm had been brewing in her absence. Her father, emitting a heavy stench of spirits, was in a froth that she was nowhere to be found. Raging he exclaimed, "A woman's place is in the house not trouncing about the woods like a dirty, backwards savage! They are a place for the wicked, like the whores from Salem!" The anger and venom in his words made her reflexively step back out of the doorway.

Gideon rushed her, roaring, "Don't you walk away from me you ungrateful impudent child!" He grabbed the back of her head, pulling on her hair so forcefully that even with her coif on she feared he'd rip her hair out. "I'm your father and I will not be insulted by some lazy good for nothing that killed the only person I ever loved!"

He then delivered a closed fist blow to Arabia's slender and fragile stomach. His blow overwhelmed her nerves so entirely, that after the first instance of pain she went numb, she could not cry out for she had no air with which to do so. All she could do was crumple to her knees before Gideon. He picked up the switch he would use for more severe discipline and struck her across the back nine times.

Gideon mumbled, "The next time I find you out in those Godless woods I won't be so gentle" and he stumbled back into the house and fell asleep in the back room; leaving Arabia a heap in the doorway, silent tears streaming down her face. However, unbeknownst to either of them, they had been watched by dark, all seeing eyes that do not forget.

A week had passed since the incident with Arabia and her father, but it was still fresh in Arabia's mind. The welts on her back faded after a couple days but every morning she had to see the disgustingly blue and purple bruising Gideon's blow had left her. She still had to feel the helplessness and humiliation of sobbing in the dirt, along with the pain every time she took in a breath. While Gideon scarcely remembered that night, Arabia's terror had never been as high as it had been this past week. She could feel the embers of her animosity starting to grow.

The only thoughts that brought her peace were of Brenna, and the joy she felt playing on that day. She had not seen the little raven since then and Arabia feared that she had forgotten her. With her father out for the day and him being almost too drunk to remember what transpired, she thought it a perfect day to try and rekindle her friendship. Arabia had decided to bring a piece of cured meat with her in hopes of re-winning Brenna's affection, and set off into the woods to find her.

The trek had been almost half the time of her first adventure, now that she knew the way. Arabia would call out Brenna's name periodically in hopes of drawing her attention, but remained unanswered. Arabia finally came to the bend in the river where she first met Brenna and decided to cry out for her friend here as loud as she could; straining through stabbing pains she felt from where her father struck her and launched her into wrenching fits of coughing.

Arabia listened for what felt like an eternity, and as she drew in breath to call again, she heard it. Faint and distant but still she recognized it as Brenna, for it was deeper than any of the cries made by crows. Arabia called again, frantically scanning the tree line for her silhouette. She could hear Brenna cry back, this time she sounded much closer.

With one last shout, Arabia saw Brenna emerge from the tree line and accelerated to her as fast as her wings could carry her. Arabia could feel her eyes watering up with delight that Brenna hadn't abandoned her. Brenna landed square on Arabia's head while Arabia greeted her by stroking the feathers on her belly.

After a moment to get them reacquainted with each other Brenna turned her head in the direction she came and cried out three times. Arabia soon saw three large dark shapes glide towards her and Brenna. Instead of coming straight to the pair, they began flying high above them in what Arabia almost thought was a synchronized dance. The three would soar straight up evenly spaced from each other, and then would fold their wings, turn upside down and fall a ways before unveiling them again and soaring off. They would repeat this over and over sometimes adding corkscrews or locking talons briefly. One of these birds revealed its wings over the head of Arabia; she looked on in awe because this bird's wingspan was as great as her own height! Standing there mouth agape, it dawned on her that these must be adult ravens, more specifically, Brenna's family.

Upon concluding this masterful display of acrobatics, the three new ravens landed to get a better summary of this strange new girl. Arabia was awestruck by the beauty and grace of the new ravens; the largest of them stood almost three feet in height, reaching just above Arabia's waist. This raven was closer to the size of a small bald eagle than it was the other ravens, and Arabia assumed this must be the leading male of the group. He had a slightly hooked beak and seemed to exude an uncanny confidence as he examined Arabia.

The next raven Arabia noticed had the most gorgeous feathers she had ever seen. They seemed to both absorb the sunlight and reflect it simultaneously; giving her an air of radiance that almost made Arabia envious. Her feathers were so smooth and well kept that they looked like a shimmering blue carapace, and practically emanated an aura as regal as her oversized mate. Her beak didn't have the hook like the larger one, yet still looked as sharp as Arabia's sewing needle.

The last raven Arabia noted was also the furthest away from her. This raven seemed distrustful of Arabia, but when he turned his head revealing his right side she soon realized the reason for his aloof nature. His right eye was a pale milky blue and had a visible scar running vertically down it, as if he had been cut long ago. His feathers were ragged and ruffled, making him appear more savage and a veteran of hardships. Arabia would have pitied him if it weren't for the way his undamaged eye watched her. His gaze felt more like a wolf stalking her through a thicket of trees than a raven.

After taking in the sight of her new company Arabia finally greeted them, "Hello! I'm called Arabia; it's a pleasure to meet Brenna's family!" Arabia's mouth hung agape with surprise as the large and beautiful ravens both responded in turn, *"Hello,"* the pair of them sounding eerily human. Arabia was both unsettled but slightly amused. The idea that these two birds seemed to have more vocabulary than her father brought a small laugh out of her, and she felt a faint smile come over her.

As the new ravens came closer to Arabia she thought it would be a good time to share some of the cured meat she brought. She gave a fingertip sized piece to Brenna, who gleefully played with it before devouring it whole. The large raven took his piece in his beak and gave Arabia a small bow before eating, and the beautiful raven did the same as the large raven however, she washed her beak in the river briefly after eating. The wolfish raven remained where he was simply observing. Perplexed, Arabia decided to advance closer to try and give him his piece, but was met with an aggressive series of croaks and wing flaps. She tossed the wolfish raven's piece at his feet and moved away slowly to give him his space.

Arabia was pondering what the most fitting names for the trio would be, while sharing more of the salted treat she had brought. The largest of the ravens had such an aura of royal elegance to him. Only one name came to her mind that seemed fitting, a name that, if she was remembering correct, was reserved for a raven of the ruling class-- Waldrom. Arabia addressed him by his newly given name, and to her glee he repeated the name back with an essence of pride. "*Waldrom!*", "*Waldrom!*", "*Waldrom!*"

With more confidence in her ability to bestow names, she moved on to the beautiful raven. She remembered old tales of the Giant King Bran and his sister Branwen and how her beauty was unrivaled. She asked the beautiful raven her thoughts on this name, to which the raven cried, "*Branwen!*", "*Branwen!*", "*Branwen!*"

Arabia grinned from ear to ear hearing the ravens repeat their names back to her in agreement. She now turned her attention on to the final raven who was eyeing the situation before him with disdain. Arabia slowly approached the wolfish raven, offering him a rather large piece of the meat she had torn off. She was roughly seven feet away when he croaked in protest. Arabia stopped and proceeded to simply reaffirm that she meant him no harm and he can come to her when he was ready for a treat. After what seemed like ages of the wolfish raven surmising if he can trust her or not, he exploded, snatching the meat out of her hand. He took to a nearby rock to savor his delicacy, ravenously swallowing the prize. Arabia knew it would take time for this one to trust her as the other ravens did, but as she watched him devour his portion it came to her. Softly and with a hint of a smile she whispered, "Wolfram, the wolf raven."

The sun was hovering just above the horizon when Arabia divided what remained of the cured meat amongst the four ravens and bid them farewell. She made certain to keep an eye on the sun this time, so as not to incur her father's wrath again. Arabia gave a look back only to find the river bend void of the raven family. Slightly hurt by the unceremonious departure she turned her sights to home and walked on.

Taking in the cool air of the forest, Arabia could sense the domineering warmth that filled September would surely break soon, now that October had arrived. While elated to be done with the heat she was worried how a winter trapped with her father would unfold. His temper had been getting worse and he bore no remorse when he had gone too far. She knew she should honor, respect, and love thy father, but in truth these were all absent when Arabia dwelled on him. She often felt she would have fared better in life had it been him rather than her mother who died.

Arabia was so deep in her brooding that she didn't realize she was back in the village till she was almost home, although what truly broke her trance was a familiar yet unexpected croak. She saw Brenna, Branwen, Waldrom, and even Wolfram all roosting on top of her house. With the sun almost gone their details were lost in the dark, giving the four of them a foreboding, and slightly dreadful silhouette that made Arabia think of the four horsemen. As she was taking in all this however, she noticed a figure begin to approach her home. Arabia knew at once it was her father and she begged the ravens to flee before Gideon arrived. They simply stared back at her tilting their heads from side to side.

Suddenly there was a loud *RACK* that rang through the air. Arabia turned to see her father hurling stones at the ravens screaming that he'll have no devil birds in his presence. The raven family avoided the stones with an ease and elegance only they seemed capable of harnessing. Taking to a nearby tree they screeched back at Gideon, *"Devil, devil,"* before flying off. Upon hearing the ravens speak Gideon ceased his rampage and for a moment he betrayed his deeper emotions. Arabia saw a flicker of something in his face that she had never seen in him before, but she knew its face all too well. She saw fear in her father for the first time.

※

Gideon didn't speak a word till the next morning. He was sitting down to break his morning fast with Arabia, and she could see her father was still deeply disturbed by the ravens. "Arabia, do you know much about those birds?" Gideon asked

"Me? No, not really. Why do you ask father?" she nervously replied.

"Well in the story of Noah, the raven failed to bring back proof of land as instructed by both Noah and God. He was distracted feasting on the wicked that drowned in the flood and for this the raven was cursed with black feathers. Now it's usually a witch's familiar or the herald of death. I saw them when your mother died and I didn't believe then. I shan't make that mistake twice."

Apprehensively, Arabia asked, "Wh-what do you have planned?"

Gideon turned his distant gaze over to her, "If they come near here again, I'll have to kill them before their wickedness spreads."

Arabia's heart sank in her chest; she knew her father would mangle any of the birds if he had even half a chance. Arabia couldn't allow her raven companions to follow her home anymore, but how could she ever make them understand?

Arabia didn't venture into the forest for several days for fear the ravens would make the fatal mistake of coming home with her, but her loneliness was consuming her from the inside. She had never fully noticed the pain before meeting Brenna and her family. She knew it had always been there but the thought that the joy she had been feeling recently may have to end, made her realize just how alone she truly was. She had been silently crying herself to sleep, agonizing over if it would be safe to pay them at least one more visit. It wasn't till the third night of this impasse that she decided she would make one last venture to see the ravens. Now that October was almost half over everyone could feel winter's grasp slowly engulfing them and Arabia knew she couldn't make the journey in the snow. She decided that in the morning she would set out for a final visit.

It was a chilly overcast morning and Arabia was sluggish in her morning routine; her thoughts were simultaneously heightened and distorted. She knew it was her duty to honor and respect her father, yet her unacknowledged fury was growing too difficult to subdue. It took every ounce of Arabia's will to keep a calm surface till Gideon left for the day. She lingered for around half an hour; till she was sure her departure wouldn't be noticed by him. Despite the fact she brought no provisions (out of fear the food was causing the ravens to follow her home) Arabia felt as if she was weighed down by a dozen heavy chains. Every step she took felt as if she was knee deep in mud and the cold air stung her face and throat as she trudged onward. Due to the pain and the cold, doubt began to rear its ugly face in Arabia's mind. *How could some dumb girl make birds understand her? What if they follow her again and she inadvertently gets them killed by her father? Maybe she deserves to be alone.* Then as if hearing Arabia's thoughts, a comforting cry came from her friend Brenna, and just for a moment Arabia completely forgot about her fears and worries. Arabia rushed to the usual meeting place and found Brenna soaring high in the sky while Waldrom and Branwen took turns folding their wings in and diving to the ground; correcting themselves at just the last second, while Wolfram remained perched in a tree observing. Arabia bellowed out their names in delight, "Brenna! Woldrom! Branwen! Wolfram!"

They each came in to greet Arabia; Brenna landed on her head giving a, *"Hello!"* Branwen landed on her outstretched arm, Woldrom being the largest simply stood by Arabia, and Wolfram moved to a closer tree for a better view of the young girl. Arabia was filled with glee at having her friends by her side again, yet her heart ached over the thought of this being the last time she received a welcome as warm as this. Despite Arabia beaming upon being reunited she began to weep heavily.

Arabia sank to her knees, tears streaming down her face, "Oh my dearest friends, I don't know how to convey any of this to you but my father wishes to see you all dead! It's no longer safe for you to come home with me and I fear with the first snow almost here I shan't be able to traverse the forest to see you much longer." Arabia sobbed and trembled as she spoke. "In truth I fear this may be our final time in each other's company and I don't know if I can bear that loneliness again." The ravens looked at Arabia with the naiveté of a child, unable to discern the meaning in her words, or the strange noises she emitted. However Arabia's words and turmoil would be secondary, as no fewer than thirty small dark figures flooded the tree branches and commenced encircling the five of them.

Their cries which were harsher and higher than the ravens, created a symphony of frustration and the intention to take their grievances out on the five intruders. The unfolding scene broke through Arabia's veil of sorrow and replaced it with fear. The crows swarmed just above the trees coming together in a manner that made them appear as one single furious entity. Arabia remained frozen in awe and terror by the spectacle before her. Her trance broke only when she heard the bone chilling howl of a wolf. Panic filled Arabia, and then all at once Wolfram and Waldrom took flight towards the dark mass of crows as Branwen instinctively escorted Brenna to the tree line, leaving Arabia confused and shaking with terror. The mass of crows dove to meet the two ravens; despite Wolfram being the size of three crows and Waldrom closer to four or five, their sheer numbers quickly overwhelmed the mighty pair, forcing them to retreat closer to the ground, speeding in the direction of Arabia only half aware of the oncoming peril.

Waldrom rushed past Arabia with such power, she could hear the air part for him, with Wolfram following close behind. Frantically evading the attacks of the front most members of the crow mass. Before Arabia could process what was happening, the crow mass was upon her. Their small yet sharp beaks pierced through her wool and flesh with ease, sending Arabia into a frenzy. She flailed her arms every which way, striking a few crows but the mass persisted. Arabia bolted for the woods in the hopes that the trees might limit their numbers. She endured the sting of their jabs with every step, yet she was fast approaching her limit for pain and her fear. While the trees prevented the mass from fully overwhelming Arabia she still found herself pursued by five determined members. Having run till she could no longer run, she dropped to the cold floor of the forest. The crows continued to peck and scratch at her without remorse, and with no sign that they would stop, Arabia snapped.

That animalistic outrage sprang forth in a way she had never felt before; in one swift movement she grabbed a nearby fallen branch and swung with all her might striking one of the crows. With a small yet sickening *crunch* the bird fell to the ground, unmoving aside from a small spasm in its left leg. This removed all sense of boldness from the remaining four and they quickly left to find the main mass. Arabia wrapped up in her fury went to make sure she finished her foe, until she saw the damage she had already done. The small bird's right side had been shattered by her blow, leaving the head twisted in an unnatural position. The image of this crumpled crow sent

Arabia to times when she herself was just a heap on the ground. Arabia's own brutality caused her to weep in self loathing. She wanted so desperately to make things right but she knew there was no going back. So consumed by her grief she failed to notice the snow had begun.

Arabia silently carried the body of the small crow in a trance like fashion to the clearing where the whole ordeal started. She plodded along mindless to her own injuries and surroundings. She had only acknowledged her arrival after tripping on a tree root as she exited the forest. Arabia was met with a fuming ruckus from the mass of crows that had now encircled the clearing in its entirety. Their calls were legion and filled with disdain, and Arabia knew she had earned every bit of it. She slew one of their family members and she could never atone for it, but she would do what little she could to correct things. Through the crows unknowable jeers and curses she proceeded to dig a small grave for the poor creature. She ornamented its feathers with a stunning white flower she found near the edge of the forest and its grave with smooth black stones she found near the river.

Arabia lowered the crow into the makeshift grave as delicately as a mother would lower a child into a crib. As she did so, she started to cry again, "I'm so sorry, I didn't mean to intrude in your home, nor did I wish to harm you in such a manner! Everything just happened so fast, I'm so terribly sorry!"

Her clear empathy brought the crows to stillness; they examined her with a weary calmness unsure if it was yet safe to approach. It was only when Arabia finally could cry no more that the first crow came in for a better look. The crow was petite with an almost childlike stature in comparison to the ravens, yet had the same intelligent and knowing look in its eye. It looked the scene up and down, and then it would look from Arabia to the vanquished crow and back again. This continued for a couple minutes till suddenly it took off to the river stopping by the bank and returning with a stone of its own, placing it in the grave. Then another crow followed suit, and another, and another, before long every crow was depositing stones to seemingly pay respects. Arabia knelt by the grave in awe of what she had started amongst the crows, they had in almost no time at all filled their friend's grave with stones from the river and were standing silently giving their condolences.

The silence lingered for what felt like a lifetime, until it was broken by a voice Arabia had never heard before, "Jesus said unto her, *'I am the resurrection and the life: he that believeth in me though he were dead yet shall he live. And whosoever liveth, and believeth in me, shall never die: Believest thou this? John 11:25-26.'*"

Arabia scrambled to her feet in a panic, causing the crows closest to her to scatter in a huff. Before Arabia, stood an elderly Native American man, his hair was almost an identical jet black to Arabia's, aside from some gray forming at the temples, yet was significantly longer than hers and adorned with an eagle and two raven feathers. He was shorter than her father and had a slim yet toned build. His face had only the earliest signs of aging but his light brown eyes portrayed a deep seeded wisdom that was only acquired through many life experiences. He wore moccasins that appeared to be crafted by his own hand; along with britches made from the hide of some great beast.

However what Arabia found odd was that his wool jacket, despite being worn and patched with bits of animal hides, was clearly of puritan tailoring. He carried a satchel around his right shoulder, a bow on his left shoulder, and a tomahawk on his left hip. Arabia tried to show confidence in her stance, yet was visibly trembling. The stranger gave her a warm smile and asked her, "Well child, *do* you believe?" Arabia was struck dumb by not just his question, but also his almost contradictory nature. He looked essentially like the description of a savage she had been warned about for years, yet he had knowledge of scripture and a gentle presence that made her feel unusually trusting.

With hesitation in her voice, "Be-Believe in what exactly? And why should I answer a stranger such as you?"

"Forgive me young one, my puritan name is Mordecai, but my name of birth is Nanepashemet, and I was curious if you believe that with God resurrection is possible." Smiling as he looked upon the frightened young girl.

Arabia was stunned, both by his question and his declaration of being puritan. After she had taken a few moments to comprehend the entirety of the situation she finally spoke, "Well I'm Arabia. As to your question I believe Jesus was resurrected, but I was told my mother had more faith than anyone yet she never was resurrected." Tears were welling up in Arabia's eyes, "She believed in God, but he didn't see fit to let us have even a day together! He left me all alone with that disgusting miserable old bear!" Arabia had seemingly lost sight of the original question and had begun to sob uncontrollably.

The old Native American man slowly approached Arabia, knelt down and gave her a hug for comfort. This shocked Arabia out of her spiral, initially wanting to recoil but after a couple moments she returned the embrace.

The hour had grown late and the snows were already knee deep when Nanepashemet decided to make camp in a cave deep enough for shelter, though it was too low in height for him to stand wholly. It was upon his insistence Arabia stayed to wait out the snow storm and have her wounds tended to. While she was grateful for the hospitality her fear was ever present, for she knew her father would be furious with her. The panic over the punishment she would receive in the morning was seeping into every part of her, a fact that didn't go unnoticed by Nanepashemet. "What has you so frightened, child?" he asked with genuine concern.

"My father, the last time I was out in the forest late into the night he punished me severely…. I had hoped to say farewell to my friends, but now I fear for both their safety and my own." replied Arabia, tears beginning to form in her eyes again. Nanepashemet nodded with a noticeable look of concern.

"I can feel your fear child, and I understand the pain you go through. However I want you to know you're braver than you know. I saw how you protected the Unkindness from the Murder. It was truly worthy of awe." He said softly and with sincerity.

Arabia gave him a flattered but puzzled look, "What do you mean I protected an unkindness from being murdered?"

Nanepashmet chuckled and smiled at this question, "Young Arabia, a group of ravens is an Unkindness or a Conspiracy. The Murder I refer to is what a large group of crows is named. In fact it was the gathering of the two that brought me to you."

Nanepashmet's expression seemed to darken and grow hollow and distant. Arabia was unsure what had come over him and was steadily becoming concerned for the blizzard had become too severe for her to traverse home alone. She began to feel trapped when Nanepashmet finally spoke," You've been remarkably kind to share some of your story with me and I'd like to repay that kindness. If you care to listen I'd like to share my own story with you." Arabia nodded with a hint of trepidation. "Very well, I was born in a time of change. My elders sensing the impending change sought to create a bond with the ever expanding Puritans. Allowing one of them to stay amongst us teaching him our language and customs; in turn we would learn his. This man was named John Elliot, and he was a kind and understanding man. An unfortunate rarity I would find out later in life."

He paused for a moment, letting the memories of his youth flutter across his face before resuming. "He negotiated with our elders to found the town Natick in 1651, building it on one of our traditional holy places; some believe it to be the original birthplace of the Wampanoag. We all decided it was the best way to create a new and lasting bond between our people. The town would be of Puritan faith and adhere to Puritan traditions, but it was seen as a rebirth for the Wampanoag and surrounding tribes; a means to continue an age of peace and prosperity. The first Bible ever printed in this land was in my people's language, the Algonquian language. It was the first time anything had been written in our tongue, and within the first two years John Elliot had taught over a hundred of us to read and write using the Bible he created, myself included. I was thirteen when Natick was founded and was given the name Mortecai."

Nanepashmet seemed to have a prideful tone in his voice as he reminisced. Smiling slightly he continued his story. "The Praying towns as they would come to be called lived in an odd shade of gray between the two communities. Never being fully accepted by either, nevertheless we would try to broker peace when tensions would rise. A task which was manageable with Massasoit as Chieftain, however upon his death in 1661 things became steadily worse between my two people. By this time I had been raised more as a Puritan than Wampanoag as had my new family, my wife who bore the names Chepi and Priscilla and my daughter who we named Delilah. We were seen as outsiders to my Wampanoag brothers and sisters, especially when Massasoit's son Metacomet, also known as King Phillip, became Chieftain in 1662. I feared that soon neither side would care for our talks of peace and mutual benefit, and would soon see us an enemy. It was in 1675 when my fears would come to fruition."

Nanepashmet closed his eyes and inhaled deeply, holding the cold blizzard air in his lungs for sometime before letting it out slowly with a cloud giving him a slight ethereal look. His mood was clearly darkening when he continued his story "It was June 24th when King Phillip declared war along with three other tribes in the area. Having been mistreated and encircled by the settlers the Wampanoag and other tribes had finally reached their breaking point. They set off destroying homesteads and property held by Puritans. The Puritans began to succumb to fear with each passing day and became increasingly hostile. Finally during a cold October, much like this one now, our fellow Puritans forced us from our homes with nothing more than our day clothes and marched us to Deer Island, believing we were aiding King Phillip and his men. We had signed multiple treaties stating our neutrality, but in the eyes of our Puritan peers we were still savages in suits. Our stay on Deer Island was a horrendous expression of barbarity; they forbade us from making fires even on the coldest of winter nights. We couldn't erect shelter, or hunt to feed and clothe our families. My poor daughter… she couldn't keep her strength up no matter how hard Priscilla and I tried. My darling Delilah died early that November, she had just turned fourteen."

With tears starting to pour down Nanepashmet's wrinkled face; Arabia felt he looked ancient and tired; her heart went out to him and gave him a gentle reassuring touch on his arm. He clasped her hand and gave her a small smile, "I appreciate your kindness; you have a similar spirit to my Delilah. She had a knack for helping others." This sentiment warmed Arabia's heart more than any fire she had known, bringing a wide tooth filled smile to her face. Nanepashmet gave a gentile half smile that quickly dissipated. He paused for a second then began to stare out into the blizzard.

With the exception of the winds whistling through the cave, it was silent for what felt like hours to Arabia; being unable to bear the silence she asked,"What happened to Priscilla?"

Without making eye contact he replied," I'm not sure; slavers would frequent the island and only a few weeks after Delilah passed they took her and sold her to some islands farther south than I could manage to venture. I lost the will to live after that. I abandoned what little food was available; I starved myself for almost two weeks. It was only after witnessing John Elliot, now an old man, had been capsized by his fellow Puritans for bringing us food and blankets that my humanity returned. Having lost most of my strength, I could only watch helplessly as he flailed and struggled in the water, and I saw only he could pull himself out. It was then I knew this was not God's will but instead the true face of the Devil. The Puritans were so frightened of the 'Red Devils' that they forgot the truest face of Lucifer is that of an angel. In believing they were doing God's work they had in actuality been committing an ocean of sins, outweighing any of the evils that they sought to destroy."

Arabia found herself at a complete loss of words. She had been told all her life that the Natives were savages who would collect scalps for trophies, worship evil Gods, and eat raw animals. However what Nanepashmet was telling her about her people's crimes sounded like the description of a Hell she only heard of in her Bible lessons. She couldn't understand how anyone could endure such a thing let alone have any ability to smile after such a reality, "Ho-how could you not wither under such circumstances, much less find joy in life?"

Nanepashmet closed his eyes tight, in an attempt to stifle his mourning, "At first dear girl it was pure spite. I hated the puritans for betraying us, I hated my people for not rising up sooner and letting us be taken away, but more than anything I hated God... I hated God for letting his children do this to each other and abandoning us all. However I hadn't realized the descent into my Hell was not yet over. As I began to eat again I had trouble keeping it down but slowly my stomach strengthened and I became ravenous. I would eat as much as I could and I didn't care how I obtained the food, I would steal, cheat, or even beat my fellow prisoners just for an extra mouth full of bread. In the summer of 1676, when Puritan victory seemed imminent they cut back on our rations even more. The dead were more plentiful than anything else on the Island and I felt the spirit of the Wendigo take me as it was taking others."

Arabia's stomach churned at the thought of being desperate enough to eat a person, giving a small grimace as she listened. "It was then the crows and ravens began to come in mass. At first we were disgusted when they started eating our fallen, but we knew in our hearts we were soon to do the same, then the disgust soon turned inward. I swore on the memory of my daughter I wouldn't allow myself to become an abomination. I ate just the minimum to survive for several months. I had cruelly hoped that when King Philip had been killed that August that the Puritans would see mercy and release us, unfortunately they didn't share that belief. It took John Elliot pleading and protesting with the community leaders for months before they finally allowed us freedom, but by then over half of us on the island had died and most of us survivors we were left destitute and homeless for the Puritan victors took a third of our towns as compensation for their lost land during the war. So I wandered afterwards, trying to find meaning to all of it and struggling to keep hatred out of my heart."

Arabia looked at Nanepashmet with admiration and melancholy. She could never have imagined something so horrendous could happen to people let alone in God's name. She felt a hollowness begin to fill her, a bubbling cauldron of icy black molasses that seemed to chill her to her very soul. Arabia's eyes brimmed with tears as she spoke to Nanepashmet, "I can't even express how much remorse I have for how you and your family were treated. I'm so sorry…" Nanepashmet gave Arabia a soft smile and pulled her in for a hug.

"It's not your sin to bear, sweet child. It rests solely on the shoulders of the ones who let fear overtake their hearts." He then began to sing softly to Arabia in a language she had never heard before. Arabia slowed her breathing; it felt as if in that moment time was slowed. The howls of the wind whipping across the cave, the small crackling warmth of the fire, and the sweetly sad sound of Nanepashmet's song. The trinity of these simultaneous events made her feel such a deep sense of content that she didn't even feel herself slip into slumber.

※

Arabia awoke the next morning to the soft shake of Nanepashmet stirring her. He spoke to her in a soft and comforting voice, "It seems the snow has stopped for the time being. I think we should break our fast and I'll guide you back to your village." At the mere thought of returning home Arabia started trembling, far more than the frozen jabs of the blizzard had made her.

"I… I'm scared…. My father was very angry when I was out late in the woods and I know he'll be furious this time." Nanepashmet looked at her with sorrow and understanding,

"There is no need to fret little one, I'll see to it you return to your village unharmed." Arabia saw the ferocity behind his eyes when he told her this; however she also saw staleness, the kind that oxen get in their final days of working fields, or when her father has excessive spirits and is moments away from keeling over. Arabia smiled and did her best to quiet these intrusive thoughts.

Arabia and Nanepashmet set out on their journey to Arabia's village. The once light green pines were now towering white spires that seemed ready to release a payload of their accumulated frozen vapor. It gave Arabia restless unease that she couldn't explain, however as she saw four dark shapes in the sky above her feelings soon shifted to elation! The ravens swooped and twisted in the air; flipping upside down and crying out *"Hello!" "Hello!"*

With tears forming (and ever so slightly freezing) in her eyes she cried back, "Hello my beautiful friends, oh how I feared the worst for you all but you're all safe!" Each of the four ravens landed for Arabia; Brenna took her usual spot on top of Arabia's head, Branwen chose to perch on her left shoulder, Waldrom hopped his massive body alongside Arabia, and even Wolfram touched down within petting distance of the young girl, watching her warily with his good eye. Nanepashmet looked at the sight of this young girl whose skin could almost blend into the icy blanket that now enveloped the earth, whose hair appeared as radiantly black as the very ravens that roosted beside her, and had the sense he was bearing witness to something celestial.

They were nearly a quarter of a mile away from the village when Nanepashmet spoke, "Do you know why the raven turned black?"

Arabia had a hollow sorrow in her voice as she said, "My father said it was because God and Noah cursed them for not finding proof of land and favored eating the dead..."

Nanepashmet nodded slightly, "After my time on the island I started to think that they ate the dead not out of gluttony or greed, but they were instead trying to prevent the sins of the past from taking root in the hearts of the future. For how can you reap a pure harvest when it's sown in fields of sin? It's my firm belief that the raven sought only to remove the sins of humanity for us to truly start anew; thus earning the black color from taking on more than it could bear." Arabia had never considered that before. She looked at Brenna playfully nipping at Branwen as she swooped and twisted in the air; she watched Woldrum and Wolfram soaring high above keeping an ever present eye on them and she knew in her heart the birds couldn't possibly have wickedness in them.

Smiling Arabia said, "You know, I think I agr-," *CRACK!*

Arabia quickly spun to her left and saw Nanepashmet was bleeding from the back of his head. Whipping around in a confused panic she saw a big bear of a man, and as the second stone was let loose she knew, it was her father.

As the second stone smashed into Nanepashmet's right clavicle Gideon roared, "SAVAGE! How dare you show your dirty red face around here? Get your mongrel hide away from my damned daughter!" While Nanepashmet stood reeling in pain Gideon began to charge, axe in hand.

Frantically Arabia stepped in the way desperately pleading with Gideon to stop, "Father no! He's a good man!" Unfortunately she was met with a face splitting back fist. In Arabia's mind it felt almost as if she was floating to the ground watching all of this horror far away, far from even her own body.

She heard strange faint voices, they sounded like they were saying, *"DEVIL! DEVIL! DEVIL!"* as three large black shapes descended in succession one after the other, striking Gideon in the face and head drawing blood with each pass. Arabia slipped into unconsciousness as Nanepashmet drew his tomahawk. Arabia slowly came back to her body, first she felt the searing pain in her right cheek, next came an oddly disturbing *BLAP, BLAP, BLAP,* sound.

Arabia slowly rose looking for the source of the noise as her stomach dropped. Nanepashmet lay on the ground with Gideon straddling his chest, indefinitely raining heavy fists into Nanepashmet's face. Arabia's horror had become too great for her to govern, when she felt a familiar inferno smolder inside her. She saw Gideon had lost his axe not far from where Arabia had fallen. With burning, cold, and trembling hands she picked up Gideon's axe and slowly approached the massive beast. Arabia had the presence of mind to turn the blade around to strike with the dull end; Gideon was so preoccupied with his mauling that he remained unaware of Arabia.

Summoning every drop of her rage Arabia swung the blunt side of the axe into Gideon's skull, and with a sickening *CRUNCH* caved in his left temple. Gideon fell to the right and immediately started to convulse and froth foam from the mouth. Arabia, despite deeply loathing her father, the sight of him gasping for a breath he couldn't take, twisting in an inhuman way, and seeing nothing but white voids in his eyes brought her to tears, filling her with disgust for her own existence. As her father took his last pitiful spasms Arabia looked at Nanepashmet's broken and distorted face and knew she had been too late to even save her friend, she dropped to her knees and bellowed a hate filled wail.

Arabia knelt in the snow, unaware of how much or if any time had truly passed. Staring at the shimmering crimson that stained the snow, she barely even felt present, as if everything was miles and miles away. Although deep down she knew it was right in front of her and there was no going back. Arabia was so lost in herself she hadn't noticed Wolfram pecking at Gideon's eye, or the disturbed crowd that had begun to form around her. One bold on looker tried to ask Arabia what had happened but she found herself unable to answer. Regrettably Wolfram, whose beak was scarlet tipped, took up the response for her, "*Devil! Devil!*"; sending the herd of people into fearful murmurs of witchcraft. Arabia barely reacted as the mob of people gently took her away.

※

Several days had passed since the incident in the woods, and the village that Arabia grew up in was certain in their belief that she had been possessed by Indian magic when she murdered her father and clearly had ravens as familiars. Some spread tales of her laughing incessantly when they found her dripping in the men's blood. Others claimed she was in the shape of a raven trying to flee until the Lord's Prayer forced her into human form.

Arabia, locked up in a cage that was an undersized fit for a grown man, yet seemed comically large for a child, was unable to defend her reputation. Not that it would have done much; the village folk had a deep fear and mistrust of any native and would dismiss her defense as poisonous babble from a witch. Arabia had heard of what befell the victims of Salem and had a feeling she would be joining them in this destiny, yet this didn't bring her the despair she thought it would. It was quite the opposite in fact, she was accepting of her fate for she knew the truth and that would matter more to God than the people. She hoped this would still be true come her day of judgment.

The inescapable day was finally upon the gentle Arabia. The village brought her to the center square of town in front of the church, however instead of an open dirt field there now stood a tripod type structure with a pulley and a noose threaded through it. This newly erected device gave Arabia the strongest sense of deja vu and she was starting to feel panicked. She was muttering, "No, no, no, no, no," to herself until she saw them. Four large black figures watching the ugly sight before them with a harsh eye, yet the sight of her friends gave her a warm comfort and she let a soft smile come across her face. Arabia was brought before the tripod watching the crowd, some had frightened expressions, others seemed hateful, or gazed at her like she was grotesque.

The preacher came before her, a tall slender man with frosty blue eyes and a hooked nose, whose features looked almost stone like. He spoke half to Arabia and half to the crowd, "You stand accused of consorting with the

Devil, witchcraft, and murder by no less than ten of these good people, how do you plea?"

Arabia stared at her feathered friends for sometime before giving her response, "I saw no Devil in those woods, I never learned a single spell, however I did slay my father... He was a beast in a human's skin but he was still my father. I will accept whatever punishment God sees fit for me."

The preacher gave a small disapproving grimace, "So do you confess or deny your crimes?"

Arabia responded to the preacher with ferocity in her face, "I did kill my father, in order to protect my friend. It wasn't my intention to kill him but it was God's will. He was drunk and cruel but killing him didn't take away my pain and hanging me won't get any of you into heaven. You've all let your fear overtake you and in the process damned yourselves." The crowd began to angrily grumble at her words.

The preacher stepped in at this point, "That's quite enough out of you! Arabia it is by our Lord and savior's will that you hang from the neck till dead. May God have mercy on your soul." At this there was the howl of a wolf as Wolfram swooped down and began a violent assault on the preacher's face, pecking and clawing till the preacher shook him off. When the mauling was done the preacher seemed as if he was crying tears of blood from where Wolfram clawed him.

While the attack was taking place Brenna had come down to give Arabia a final few moments of comfort by nuzzling her and making soft croaking sounds. The crowd went into an uproar chanting, "WITCH! WITCH! WITCH!" At this the preacher asked for volunteers to man the rope, to which nine people stepped forward.

The preacher placed the noose around Arabia's neck and with a single solid heave Arabia was lifted high into the air gasping and flailing for oxygen. Time seemed to slow as she felt the noose bite into her skin, drawing blood, but soon the pain dulled as the world slowly faded to black.

They left Arabia's body to hang in the square for an entire day. In Salem some witches would continue to hang for a week or more but the village felt it gratuitous for a child, and they were unnerved by how her ravens refused to leave her. The ravens stared at each and every villager with omnipresent, wrathful, and ever so slightly hungry eyes. It was forbidden to bury convicted witches in Christian graveyards so two men were tasked to bring Arabia's body deep into the woods, a chore that the village was eager to have done.

Her body was loaded into a wagon and taken a few miles deep into the woods, where the two men promptly threw her cold petite remains down a snow bank, rolling till she came to rest on her back. The men hurriedly struck out back to the village, as the ravens, who had not let Arabia's corpse out of their sight, proceeded to land on Arabia and croak softly to her. Brenna nuzzled Arabia's cheek unable to understand why she wouldn't giggle back to her like she normally would. Branwen and Woldrom were hopping about in a puzzled and distressed manner, and Wolfram went against his aloof nature and was right next to Arabia's face letting out a bemoaned wolfish howl.

The ravens were so deep into their grief that they hadn't noticed the murder of crows that was gathering watching events unfold. However they were uncharacteristically calm, sad even, they too knew the kindness of Arabia and shared the pain the ravens felt. Slowly they each came to the small girl, who had become so pale she could easily have been lost in the snow, and started leaving trinkets. Some brought twigs, or bark, even stones from the not too far river and placed them on and around Arabia before returning to their tree top perches.

The Unkindness and Murder sat together mourning till something large caught their attention. There was a white shape forming in the sky drawing closer to this unconventional gathering, however it wasn't until it landed that the birds could see; it was a gargantuan white raven. This raven made even the regal Waldrom look like a common crow, with feathers so radiantly white it almost seemed to illuminate the snow, its eyes were as blue as the heavens, and it carried with it nine daisies.

This raven confidently yet gracefully approached Arabia, delicately and methodically placing the nine daisies in her hair. The white raven spoke in a forcefully booming voice, "Believer." and ever so softly placed the tip of its beak on the young girl's forehead pausing for a few moments before it lifted its head looking at the small group of ravens and gave them a warm croak and effortlessly took off. It looked almost immaculate as it soared away, vanishing in the snow. Brenna, Branwen, Woldrom, and even Wolfram all hopped to the young girl's body, watching for what seemed like a lifetime before she slowly opened her evening blue eyes.

Made in the USA
Las Vegas, NV
18 May 2021

23280900R00025